GOING HOME

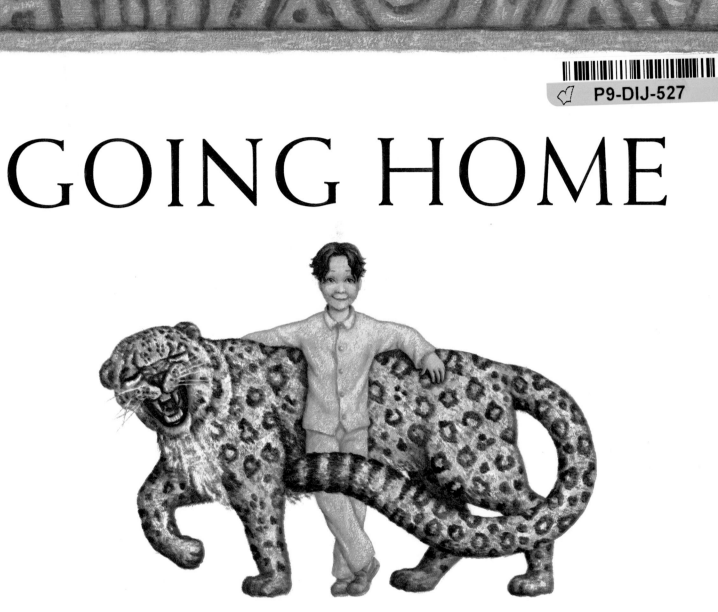

Margaret Wild • Wayne Harris

SCHOLASTIC INC.

New York Toronto London Auckland Sydney

To Donna. MW
To Mary Mellis. WH

Text copyright © 1993 by Margaret Wild.
Illustrations copyright © 1993 by Wayne Harris.
All rights reserved. Published by Scholastic Inc., 555 Broadway,
New York, NY 10012, by arrangement with Ashton Scholastic Pty Limited.
The illustrations in this book were painted with acrylics.
Printed in the U.S.A.
ISBN 0-590-47959-8

4   5   6   7   8   9   10   08   01   00   99   98

Hugo is in a small hospital
right next to the zoo.
He's much better and wants
to go home.
"Soon," says the doctor.
But how soon is soon?

"Cheer up. It won't be long now," says Nurse Benny.

"Come and play cards," says Simon in the next bed.

"This is a really good show," says Nirmala, who
watches TV all the time.

4

But Hugo shakes his head and stares out the window.
Right now Mom will be putting on the kettle, and his
little sister, Cathy, will be playing dress-up, and his fat cat,
Lucy, will be napping in the sun.

So Hugo stares out the window,
listening to the animal noises
that float up from the zoo.
"What a racket," says Nurse Benny,
but Hugo's eyes widen because an
elephant is shrieking something
special — a message just for him.

"Come, come home with me," shrieks the elephant.
So Hugo puts on his slippers — and goes.
He and the elephant amble through African grasslands,
where lions play rough-and-tumble games, and herds
of wildebeests migrate across the plains.

When his family comes to visit,
Mom asks as usual,
"What have you been up to?"

"Quite a lot," says Hugo.
"I went to Africa."

"Lucky you," says Mom.

"It's not fair!" says Cathy.
"I only went to kindergarten."

So Hugo makes her a little paper
elephant with flappy ears.

The next day while Simon is building a house
out of cards and Nirmala is still watching TV,
Hugo stares out the window and listens again.

The elephant is silent,
but the howler monkey is roaring,
"Come, come home with me."
So Hugo puts on his slippers — and goes.

He and the howler
monkey swing through
the treetops of the Amazon
jungle, where sloths sleep
upside down, and the
emerald tree boa hides in
the leaves, and toucans
gobble berries.

When his family comes to visit, Mom asks,
"Where did you go today?"

"Quite far," says Hugo.
"I went to the Amazon jungle."

"Lucky, lucky you," sighs Mom.

"It's not fair!" says Cathy.
"I only went to the corner shop."

So Hugo makes her a monkey puppet
that wiggles on her finger.

The next day, after Hugo has
played cards with Simon and
watched a bit of TV with Nirmala,
he stares out the window.
And, very faintly, he can hear
the snow leopard growling,
"Come, come home with me."
So Hugo puts on his slippers
— and goes.

He wraps his arms around
the snow leopard's neck, and they
hurtle through snow and ice
high in the Himalayas,
where eagle-eyed birds soar
above the slopes.

When his family comes to visit,
Mom asks, "Been traveling again?"

"Yes," says Hugo,
"I went to the Himalayas."

Cathy stamps her foot. "Not fair!
I only went to the park."

So Hugo makes her a leopard
mask, and she growls and shows
her claws.

The next day when Hugo is just about to put on his slippers and leave for India, Nurse Benny says, "Surprise! Your mom and Cathy are here — you're going home."

"Come back and visit me," says Simon.

"I wish I were going home, too," says Nirmala, and she watches TV harder than ever.

"I'll tell you both a secret," says Hugo,
and he whispers in their ears.

That night when Hugo is snuggled up
in his own bed in his own house at last . . .

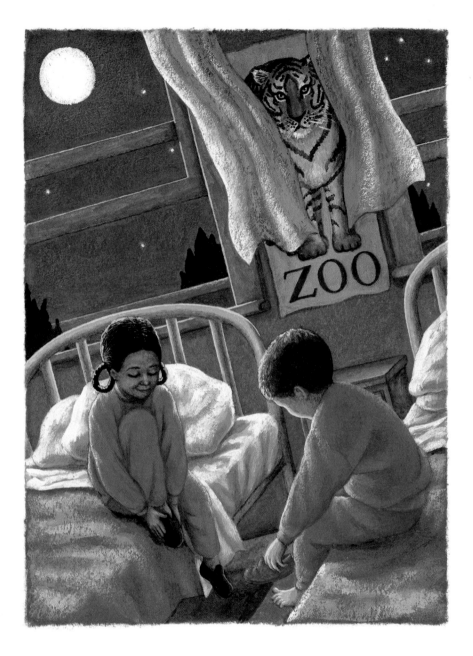

Nirmala and Simon put on their slippers . . .

and run with the tiger
through the forests of India.